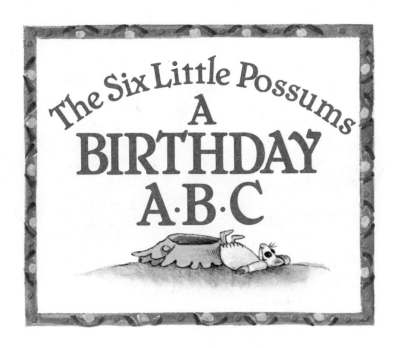

The Six Little Possums
A
BIRTHDAY
A·B·C

By Marci McGill
Pictures by Cyndy Szekeres

GOLDEN PRESS • NEW YORK
Western Publishing Company, Inc., Racine, Wisconsin

Today is Peapod's birthday.
The possums are going to have a special
birthday picnic for her.

A is for the apple Mama puts in the
picnic basket.

B is for basket and C is for cake.
Papa puts Peapod's birthday cake into
the basket.

D is for dress.

Ginger helps Peapod put on her prettiest
party dress.

"I am the birthday girl!" says Peapod.

E is for ear and F is for flower.
Sage puts a big flower behind her ear.
"Don't I look lovely?" she asks Pepper.
Pepper makes a funny face.

G is for the green grass in the meadow
where the possums will have their picnic.

H is for the hug Parsley gives Peapod
when she falls down and bumps her knee.
"Be careful, birthday girl," says Parsley.

I is for ice.

Papa puts ice on Peapod's knee to make it feel better.

"Thank you, Papa," says Peapod.

J is for jelly.

Mama is making walnut-butter-and-jelly
sandwiches for lunch.

She lets Peapod have a spoonful of jelly
as a special treat.

K is for the kiss Peapod gives Nutmeg
when he brings her some birthday flowers.

L is for lollipop.

There is a big lollipop by each little possum's plate.

"That is for after lunch," says Mama.

M is for the milk the six little possums drink with their lunch.

N is for nap.
The six little possums take a nap after lunch.
"When you wake up, we will have the party,"
says Papa.

O is for orange.

When the six little possums wake up, it's time for a snack.

Papa peels a juicy orange for them.

P is for Peapod's presents and purple punch and a perfect possum party!

Q is for queen. Today Peapod feels like a queen.

R is for the red ribbons Parsley
gives Peapod.
 "I will help you tie them in your hair,"
he says.

S is for strawberries.
"These are my present for you," says
Nutmeg. "I grew them in my garden."

T is for truck and U is for umbrella.
Ginger and Pepper give Peapod a toy truck.
Sage has made her a fern-leaf umbrella.

V is for violin.

Peapod's last present is a violin from Mama and Papa.

"I will teach you how to play it," says Papa.

W is for woods.

When Peapod has opened all her presents, the six little possums go on a treasure hunt in the woods.

Mama gives them a map to help them find the treasure.

X is for X.

X marks the spot where the treasure is buried.

Parsley digs up the treasure and finds six shiny pennies — one for each little possum!

Y is for yawns.
The little possums try to hide their yawns, but Mama and Papa see them. "Time to go home," they say.

Z is for zippers.

The six little possums have zippers on their pajamas. They zip them up and hop into bed.

"This was the best birthday I ever had!" says Peapod.